Sinbad
Legend Of The Seven Seas™

Adapted by **Mary Hogan**

DREAMWORKS®

In the stars above the earth, a trouble-making goddess was making plans to steal the Book of Peace. Eris called to Cetus, an enormous sea monster. "You know what to do," she ordered, never suspecting that someone else was also planning to steal the precious book!

"Let's get rich!" cried Sinbad, the dashing captain of the pirate ship *Chimera*. His crew attacked the royal flagship carrying the Book of Peace. Swords sparked and clanged as the soldiers tried to fight off the pirates.

Sinbad had almost reached his prize, when he saw the book's final defender—Proteus, his childhood friend and prince of Syracuse. "You're not going to steal this," Proteus said. "Not from me. The Book of Peace protects all the Twelve Cities."

"Exactly," said Sinbad. "So imagine how much *all* will pay to get it back."

Proteus wondered if his old friend had really become so selfish.

Proteus soon had other worries—Cetus wrapped its huge tentacles over the deck of his ship! Sinbad and Proteus stopped fighting each other and began fighting the creature. Working together, they stabbed the creature with the ship's wooden yardarms. As Cetus sank into the watery depths, its tentacles pulled Sinbad along with it!

Underwater, Eris approached Sinbad. Protecting him in an air bubble, she made her demand, "Get the Book of Peace and bring it to me." She showed him the star to follow to find Tartarus— her realm of chaos. Then she released Sinbad. His crew was happy to see him alive.

Proteus delivered the Book of Peace safely to Syracuse. The city celebrated its arrival with a huge party. Proteus was so excited that he even welcomed some uninvited guests—Sinbad and his men. He began to introduce Sinbad to Marina, a beautiful ambassador from Thrace, but Sinbad could not stay. "Let's get back to the ship," he told his men.

Eris was determined to get the Book of Peace and was furious that Sinbad had disobeyed her command. Magically, she disguised herself as Sinbad and stole the book. The skies over Syracuse blackened and the earth quaked. The protection of the book was gone!

A palace guard identified Sinbad as the thief! Sinbad realized that Eris had taken the book, but he could not prove it. At his trial, he was sentenced to die. But before the order could be carried out, Proteus surprised everyone. "Take me in his place," he said.

Proteus explained, "Sinbad either stole the book or he's telling the truth. Either way, he's our only hope to get it back." Sinbad had ten days to retrieve the book. If Sinbad did not return before then, Proteus would be put to death in his place.

S inbad prepared his ship to leave Syracuse—but was it to find the book or just to flee? Marina stowed away on board to make sure that Sinbad headed his ship toward Tartarus. Soon the ship faced its first challenge—the Dragon's Teeth. The narrow channel was studded with rocks and the ruins of smashed ships. Sinbad carefully steered among the jagged peaks.

Through the thickening fog, voices began to murmur, faintly then louder. "What is that?" Marina asked, worried. Sinbad did not answer. The beautiful voices had left him dazed. Now Marina saw strange watery women swimming in the water around the ship, singing out their spell. All the men on the ship were hypnotized by the Sirens' song.

Marina had to grab the wheel of the *Chimera*. Desperately, she and Spike steered among the rocks, while trying to keep the lovesick men from falling overboard in pursuit of the Sirens. Finally, crashing through a wrecked ship, Marina sailed the *Chimera* to safety.

inbad was impressed with Marina's sailing, but it was hard for him to thank her. When he saw that his crew was disappointed in his bad manners, he rudely shouted "Thank you!" at her.

The *Chimera* stopped for repairs at a small island. As the crew collected tree sap to fix the boat, the ground suddenly began to shudder and shake. The island was really a giant fish—and it was about to dive underwater! The crew raced back to the ship. Then Sinbad hooked a line over the fish and it pulled them at a dizzying speed toward Tartarus.

Eris was not through with her challenges for Sinbad. She iced the seas and sent another of her creatures after his ship. Screaming from the sky, The Roc, a gigantic bird of prey, snatched Marina and dropped her in its nest atop an icy tower. Marina could not believe it when Sinbad climbed the ice wall to her rescue. "How are we going to get down?" she asked.

Sinbad didn't know. "I'm thinking about it," he said defensively. Luckily, he was a quick thinker. Using his shield like a sled, he and Marina whooshed down the slope to the safety of their ship, while narrowly escaping from The Roc!

As the *Chimera* headed out of the ice, Marina thanked Sinbad for rescuing her. The two began talking and found out that they enjoyed the same things. "I've always loved the sea—I even dreamed of a life on it," said Marina wistfully. Sinbad knew just how she felt.

As Marina and Sinbad sailed beneath the starry skies, a strange sight met their eyes. The star they had been following floated low in the night sky before them—it was the gateway to Tartarus!

"It's the edge of the world!" cried a crewman, as the ship approached a huge cliff.

The sailors were frightened, but their captain confidently shouted his orders. He directed them to reposition the sails. "All hands to your posts and wait for my command!"

Closer and closer, the *Chimera* crept toward the steep drop-off until it began to free fall into the abyss! The sails filled with air like a parachute—*whoosh, whoosh, whoosh*—and the ship floated just beyond the edge of the ocean. Sinbad's plan had worked.

inbad and Marina swung from the ship into Tartarus. Eris emerged from the bleak landscape with one last challenge for Sinbad. "Answer a question for me. If you tell the truth, the Book of Peace is yours." But Sinbad would not believe her until she crossed her heart and gave her word as a goddess.

"If you don't get the book, will you sail for the horizon, or will you go back to die in Proteus' place?" asked Eris.

"I will go back," said Sinbad.

The ground beneath Sinbad began to shatter and Tartarus echoed with Eris' mocking laughter. She was certain he had lied.

ack in Syracuse, Proteus had run out of time. He was about to be put to death when a voice called out, "Sorry Proteus. I did my best, but it wasn't good enough." Sinbad had returned! But without the book, Sinbad's own life was in danger. Marina looked away tearfully.

Before a sword could be brought against Sinbad, a dark cloud swirled over the city. Eris had arrived and she didn't look happy.

Sinbad realized what was happening. "I didn't lie. I came back and that's why you're here. I told the truth and you promised the book."

Eris was forced to return the book. As Sinbad opened the Book of Peace, its magical protection washed over the city, leaving it safe again.

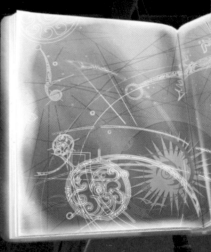

Syracuse was restored, but it could never be home for Sinbad or Marina. The seven seas were calling them to the life they loved—together.